THE RAINBOW TIGER

Gayle Nordholm

Illustrated by Jennifer Frohwerk

HARA
PUBLISHING
Seattle, Washington

Published by
Hara Publishing
P.O. Box 19732
Seattle, WA 98109
(425) 775-7868

ISBN: 1-883697-52-2
Library of Congress Number: 2001098439

Printed in Korea
10 9 8 7 6 5 4 3 2

Book Design: Lisa Delaney

This book is dedicated to my daughter, Michelle.
Through imaginary play she often transformed into "Jewel" the tiger.
When she asked for a bedtime story about tigers,
The Rainbow Tiger was born.

A special thanks to all my children.
Their desire to listen has kept my love for storytelling alive.

DEEP IN THE FORESTS OF INDIA,
there lived a beautiful tiger.
Her coat was as orange as an autumn pumpkin,
with sleek, black stripes. When she hid
in the tall grass or watched from the shadows,
the other animals could not see her.
Because of this, she was an excellent hunter
and that made her very happy.

Silently, on velvet feet, the tiger made her way through the forest each day. Listening carefully to the sounds around her, she slipped in and out of the shadows, watching for other animals.

One day, the tiger stopped at the edge of a
clearing to watch a peacock. His shimmering
feathers danced with rainbow colors as he
moved about in the sunlight.
The tiger began to imagine what it would be
like to wear such wonderful colors.
"If I had a coat of rainbow colors,"
she thought to herself,
"I'd be the most beautiful tiger ever!"

Lost in her thoughts, the tiger did not see the peacock leave the clearing. Finally, the sounds of the forest brought her back to her senses. Realizing she was alone, the tiger left the clearing and returned home.

The long walk in the heat of the afternoon
made her sleepy. A nap sounded good.
After stretching from the tip of her nose
to the very last stripe on her tail,
she rested her head and drifted off
into dreams of rainbow colors.

It seemed as though she had barely closed her eyes
when something woke her up.
Her stomach was growling loudly.
"I must have slept a long time to be so hungry!"
she thought. "I'd better go find something to eat."

Before long, she came upon a deer nibbling on some grass in the distance. The tiger lowered herself into the grass and moved forward carefully. Suddenly, the deer looked up. In a flash, she was gone.

"That deer acted like she saw me!" said the tiger. "But that's impossible! I can't be seen when I hide in the grass. Something else must have frightened her away." Too hungry to give it much thought, the tiger moved on.

After searching for some time, she heard a familiar noise. Stepping back into the shadows, she waited as a wild boar came out of the brush. He worked his way back and forth, with his nose to the ground, searching for something to eat. Slowly, the tiger moved through the shadows. The boar raised his head with a sudden jerk and looked right at her. Quickly, he spun around, and with his tail up like a flag, he ran off squealing loudly.

"How can this be happening to me?" the tiger asked. "I haven't had this much trouble since I was a cub! Maybe I'll have better luck down by the river. All this walking has made me very thirsty."

As she stepped into the river, her reflection broke into
rings of rainbow colors. Startled by the image in the water,
she saw that her coat was no longer orange as an autumn
pumpkin. Instead she wore the colors of the rainbow,
just as she had wished.

"My wish came true!" she purred with delight.
"I'm even more beautiful than I imagined!"

But as she stood there admiring her reflection,
she remembered the deer and the boar.
"So that's what happened!" she said to herself.
"They could see me when I was hiding.
Well, I'll show them! I'll be even faster
and smarter than before!"

And so the tiger leaped back up the river bank
and into the forest
with renewed determination.

Slowing her pace to a walk,
she could hear the monkeys in the trees above her.
They were chattering about something,
but she was too hungry to notice.

Just then, a light wind blew toward her,
carrying the scent of animals nearby.
Lowering herself to the ground, she prepared to spring
on anything she could find.

Suddenly, the forest broke out into laughter. The monkeys
had spread the news about a rainbow tiger down at the river.
One by one, the animals stepped forward to see her.
The peacock laughed the loudest.
"A tiger with rainbow colors! How ridiculous!"

"Now that we can see her coming,
we don't have to be afraid any more!"
the deer snickered with delight.

Embarrassed and sad, the tiger
turned away, leaving the
laughter behind her.

"Being rainbow colored isn't
so wonderful after all," she said.
"I wish I were orange and black again!"

Slowly, she made her way back home.
It had been a very long day
and she was exhausted.
"What am I going to do?"
she asked herself
as she rested in the shade.

But before she could
think any more about it,
she fell into a deep sleep.
Not even the growling
of her stomach could
wake her.

When she opened her eyes again, it was morning.
Little by little the memories returned, filling her with
sadness and regret. "Maybe a bath in the cool river will
help," she thought. "Then I'll decide what to do."

As she walked back to the river, the forest was quiet.
"The animals probably saw me coming and ran away!"
she said, feeling sorry for herself.

Stepping down into the water,
she looked at her reflection once again.
Her eyes widened in disbelief.

This time a beautiful orange tiger
with sleek, black stripes looked back at her.

"Where did the rainbow colors go?
Have I been dreaming?"

Well, to this day she's still not sure if it was real or just a dream, but she will tell you this…

"Never wish to be different than you are, because you'll never be happier than just being yourself!"

THE END

Tiger Facts

Tigers are the largest of the big cats. A large tiger can weigh almost 800 pounds. They can run fast and leap long distances, giving them the ability to catch large animals such as antelope, deer, wild pigs, and sometimes young elephants. Most tigers are active at night and do a lot of their hunting in the dark. Their night vision is six times better than humans.

You can tell tigers apart by looking at the stripes on their face and body. Just as fingerprints are unique to each person, no two tigers have the same pattern of stripes.

Tigers live in a variety of habitats — from the hot and humid jungles of Indonesia to the snowy forests of the Russian Far East. Tigers prefer to live where there is plenty of water. They often play in the water and are very good swimmers.

Today only about 5,000 - 7,000 wild tigers live across Asia. There are only five remaining subspecies. The Bali, Caspian, and Javan tigers are now extinct. The Siberian tiger lives in southeastern Russia. The South China tiger lives in southern China. The Indochinese tiger extends across most of Southeast Asia. The Sumatran tiger is restricted to the Indonesian island of Sumatra and the Bengal tiger is found primarily in India.

The tiger is a strong and resilient animal, but like all endangered animals, its habitat and food sources must be protected if it is to survive. To find out more about wildlife conservation, check for local or national agencies near you.